T5-CVE-905

The Devil and DANIEL MOUSE

By
KEN
SOBOL

AVON CAMELOT

THE DEVIL AND DANIEL MOUSE
is an original publication of Avon Books.
This work has never before appeared in book form.

"*I've Got A Song*" Music and Lyrics by John Sebastian.
Copyright © MCMLXXVIII by John Sebastian Music.
"*Concert Medley*" Lyrics by John Sebastian.
Copyright © MCMLXXVIII by John Sebastian Music.
"*Can You Help Me Find My Song*" Music and Lyrics
    by John Sebastian.
Copyright © MCMLXXVIII by John Sebastian Music.
"*Look Where The Music Can Take You*" Music and Lyrics
    by John Sebastian.
Copyright © MCMLXXVIII by John Sebastian Music.

AVON BOOKS
A division of
The Hearst Corporation
959 Eighth Avenue
New York, New York 10019
Copyright © 1979 by Nelvana Limited
Published by arrangement with Nelvana Limited.
Library of Congress Catalog Card Number: 79-51609
ISBN: 0-380-45864-0

All rights reserved, which includes the right
to reproduce this book or portions thereof in
any form whatsoever. For information address
Viacom Enterprises
1211 Avenue of the Americas
New York, New York 10036.

First Camelot Printing September, 1979

CAMELOT TRADEMARK REG. U.S. PAT. OFF.
AND IN OTHER COUNTRIES, MARCA REGISTRADA,
HECHO EN U.S.A.

Printed in the U.S.A.

Book design by Joan Walton

CONTENTS

The Devil
and Daniel Mouse

Have you ever heard of Dan and Jan? The singers? No, probably not. That was their problem. Not many people had ever heard of them.

One night, in the Porcupine Club, Jan and Dan were onstage, singing a folk song. The song went something like this:

> *Look where the music can take you*
> *When you're getting low.*
> *Look where the music can take you*
> *If you let it go.*

They came to the end and waited for the applause. But the only one left in the audience was an old frog in the corner.

"Oh, wow," Jan said unhappily. "No audience again."

Dan pointed to the frog. "Sure there is. *He* didn't leave."

"That's because he's asleep."

"Oh, well. Let's finish the show." Dan played a chord on his guitar and spoke into the mike. "We wrote this next song—"

But before he could finish the sentence, the manager jumped up. He was a fat, spiky old porcupine, with a voice like a rusty saw. "Hold it!" he shouted. "No next song! No next anything! You're fired!"

"No! You can't!" cried Jan.

"I can, too. I'm the manager. People don't want your kind of music anymore. They want to rock 'n' roll, disco, ha-cha-cha, swing it, baby, yeah man, groovy, fabulous, boogie!" Suddenly he started disco-dancing. His quills went one way and his feet another, his head jerked back and forth, his eyes rolled, and his arms flapped like wet noodles.

"Holy cow!" said Dan. "He's flipped out!"

But it was Dan and Jan who were out. Out of a job.

"From now on," the manager shouted

after them, "this is a rock club!"

Jan and Dan trudged through the cold, rainy night. They had nowhere to go, nothing to eat, and not a penny in their pockets. It looked like the end for them.

"Maybe he's right. Maybe we'd just better quit," Jan said. She felt as miserable as a wet, cold, hungry, and broke mouse could feel.

"No, come on," insisted Dan. "You gotta believe. We're gonna star someday."

"You mean starve, don't you?"

"No! Don't worry. I'll get some money."

"How?"

"You'll see. You wait right here under this tree. I'll be right back."

Jan sat down on a cold rock. She felt grumpy and annoyed and even angry. Why didn't people come to listen to them? "Ha!" she said out loud. "A star! How can you be a star without an audience?" She sniffed a loud sniffle. "If I were a rock star, then people would listen. I'd give anything to be a rock star. Anything!"

Suddenly a deep rumble began from

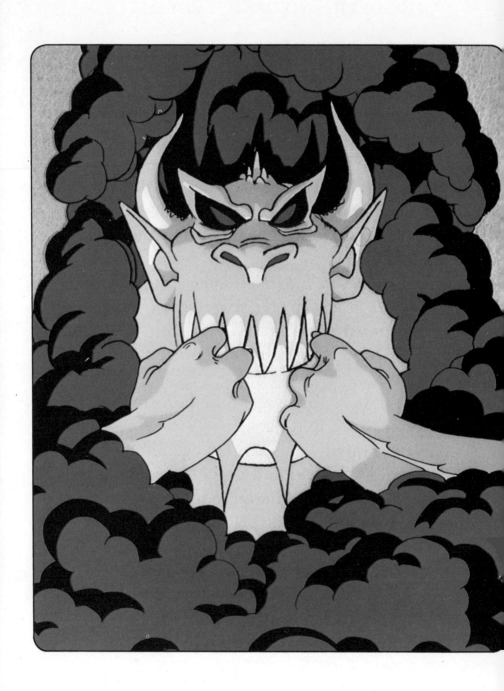

somewhere down under the ground. The earth began to shake. Trees quivered. Pebbles bounced. A huge wind blew. What was going on?

As Jan stared in amazement, a series of smoky, colored shapes popped up out of the ground. Then all at once they mixed together into one shape—a thick, clammy-looking, heavy-eyed lizard, dressed in a white suit with ruffles. The lizard stood looking down at Jan with a sly expression on his wrinkled face.

"Did you say 'anything'?" he asked.

"Who are you?"

"Zebub's the name, music's the game," he replied smoothly. "B.L. Zebub, president of Devil-May-Care Music Productions." He stuck a fat cigar in his mouth. Flames shot out from his little finger and lit the cigar. Jan just stared. "You know, kid," he went on, "I like you. Too bad you're not a singer. I'm looking for new singers."

"But I am! I am a singer!"

"Noooooooo fooling?"

"No, listen." Jan started singing. "(Look where the music)—"

"Fantastic!" interrupted B.L. Zebub. "Different! What do you think, Weez?"

At first Jan could not figure out who he was talking to. But a moment later there was another, smaller rumble from under the ground, and out popped a new creature. It looked like a mangy old weasel, all dressed up in a new green suit. And that's exactly what it was.

"She's fabulous! I love it, love it, *love it!*" the weasel screamed. "You've done it again, B.L.!"

"This is my partner, Weez Weezel," said B.L.

Jan held out her hand. But Weez was so busy snapping his fingers, jumping around, and saying "Fabulous, sensational, socko-boffo, can't miss!" that he didn't notice. "Well, anyway, pleased to meet you," Jan said.

"Far out!" cried Weez. "Out of sight! Heavy, man."

"Can you make me a star?" Jan asked.

"Heeeey, have you ever heard of the Beetles?" said B.L.

Jan was really impressed. "Wow! Did

you make them stars?"

"Naw," admitted B.L. "But that's nothing compared to how big you can be. You've
got everything it takes—looks, talent, per-
sonality. . . . There's only one thing that
could hold you back."

"What's that?"

"If you don't want it *badly* enough."

"Oh, don't worry," cried Jan. "I want to
be a star. I really want it. Please."

"You talked me into it," smiled B.L.
"Contract!" he snapped.

Weez reached into his suit pocket and
pulled out a piece of paper. A very long
piece of paper. In fact, he just kept pulling
and pulling until they were practically
buried in it.

"Listen, baby," Weez said, "this contract guarantees you fame, fortune, fans, gold
records, concerts, world tours, interviews,
movies, TV shows, and the opportunity to
meet Ronald McDonald in person. All you
have to do is sign it."

"I guess so," said Jan. But she was getting pretty mixed up. She looked around
anxiously. The woods were as empty as

before. There was no sign of Dan anywhere.

Weez finally untangled the contract, and Jan started to read it. But it was just too long.

"Oh, I give up," she said. "Can I trust you?"

All at once, B.L. put on a sweet, jolly, kindly, tender, friendly smile, which made him look exactly like Jan's favorite uncle. She had never seen anyone so trustworthy.

"Okay," she agreed. "I'll sign."

"Right!" snapped B.L. "Get the pin."

"The pin?" asked Jan.

"Oh, yeah," said B.L. His smile had grown even friendlier than before. "We always sign in blood. It's more permanent—doesn't fade. Right, Weez?"

"Oh, yeah, we do. Right on, B.L.," agreed Weez.

"Oh, I don't know. I hate blood." Jan was worried. "Couldn't we wait for Dan?"

B.L. snatched up the contract and started rolling it up. "All I want to do," he said, "is give you the chance of a lifetime, and you want to wait. Well, if that's the way you feel . . ."

"No, stop!" cried Jan. "I'll sign." She closed her eyes and held out her hand. She felt a small prick and quickly wrote her name in bright red blood. B.L.'s heavy eyes followed her finger as she wrote. The smile on his face grew wider and wider. But as it did, it changed. Now it wasn't quite so uncle-ish. It looked sort of—greedy. Like the kind of smile the Devil might have as he watched someone signing her soul over to him forever in exchange for fame and fortune.

"Give the little lady your personal attention," B.L. murmured to Weez when it was all over. "We've got to keep our end of the bargain."

"Right, B.L.!" Weez shouted. "Just stick with me, baby. You'll go places." Suddenly a puff of red smoke covered B.L., Weez, and Jan. When it cleared, they had all disappeared.

A few moments later, Dan walked up the trail, carrying a bag of groceries. He had sold his guitar—the thing he treasured most in the whole world—to get some money.

"Jan? Where are you? I've got some

food," he called.

But no answer came from the deserted woods. Only a trace of reddish mist and a faint voice whispering, "Too late, kid. She's signed with me."

The first thing Weez did was to get Jan a new look. No more patched jeans and flannel shirts for her. He gave her glittering dresses, frizzed up her hair, painted her fingernails, squeezed her into high, high, high-heeled shoes, and hung bracelets, necklaces, and rings on her until she looked like a walking jewelry store. He even got her a shiny new rhinestone-studded guitar.

Then, of course, she needed a backup band. "Watch this!" screamed Weez. He snapped his fingers, and up popped Boom Boom Beaver, the best drummer drumming, Pray Mantis, with his six arms playing a double guitar, and Rabbit Delight, the bunny bass player. What a band!

"Oh, yeah!" cried Jan. She grabbed the mike and started singing. And it came out rock 'n' roll:

Sometimes I is and sometimes I ain't.
Your sweet love honey gonna make me faint.

Wow, did I sing that? Jan asked herself. She could hardly believe it. But she liked it.

"Come on, come on," urged Weez. "We got a lot of rehearsing to do. Our first job is next week."

"Outa sight," said Rabbit Delight.

Dan came to the hall where the band was rehearsing, but Weez would not let him in. "We're featuring Jan a little—you know what I mean? You wouldn't want to spoil her chances, would you?" he asked Dan.

"No, I guess not." But Dan felt pretty lonely and left out.

Jan was too busy to notice. Before she knew it, Funky Jan and the Animal Kingdom —that was the name of her new band—were playing their first job. They were a smash! After it was over, the fans cheered for an hour. They brought her flowers, asked for autographs, and waited outside to get a look at her. She was a hit.

And that was just the start. The next day, Jan had a record contract. Soon she was number one on the charts. Her concerts were always sold out. Huge posters of her hung in kids' rooms all over the country. Her picture was on every magazine cover. You couldn't even turn on the radio without hearing her name. "Hey, all you funky, freaky people," the disc jockeys would say. "Get ready. Here they are, number one this week, next week, and every week—Funky Jan and the Animal Kingdom!"

Wow! Jan was a superstar. She had everything—fame, fortune, fans. She had gold jeans, silver sunglasses, and a diamond toothbrush. She lived in a huge mansion with fountains in front that flowed even when there was a water shortage.

One day, Dan came to visit Jan. He knocked on the door, but Weez told him Jan was busy being interviewed by a reporter from *Rolling Moss,* the famous rock magazine. "Well, just tell her I said good-bye," Dan said politely. "I'm a-traveling on." He looked up at the enormous house for a moment, then walked away.

Inside the house, Jan was in the middle of her interview.

"Tell, me, Jan, how does it feel, I mean, like, really *feel,* you know, to be a big star?" the reporter asked.

"Well, I mean, you know," Jan said, trying to think of something interesting to say,
"like being a big star is really great. Like—
uh—fabulous." Then she added, in a different voice, " 'Course, it gets lonely, too,
sometimes."

Just at that moment, Jan looked out the
window. A familiar figure was walking out
of the gate. "Was that—" she began. She
looked again. But it was too late. Dan was
gone.

But there was no time for remembering old friends. Something new had come up. Something bigger than ever. "This is it, baby!" screamed Weez. "This'll be the biggest thing ever to hit rock music!"

"What will?"

"The Roxy Halloween Marathon concert. It'll be the classiest concert of all time! The greatest gathering of the greats ever gotten on! The most sensational songfest ever suggested! The most colossal collection of—"

"Hold it! What's it got to do with me?"

"Why, Jan baby. You'll be the number one act. You're at the top now!"

"Yeah, that's true," laughed Jan. "But where do I go from here?"

"Don't worry," murmured Weez slyly. "B.L. will find someplace."

The Roxy Halloween Marathon was going to be the biggest event the rock world had ever seen. For three days the entire animal world had poured into the valley where the concert would be held. They came from the north, south, east, west, underground, and overhead. Every trail for twenty miles was crowded with creatures rushing to the great event. Swarms of bees, flocks of birds, herds of ants. All fighting for places at the concert of the century.

Finally the great night arrived. The entire valley was filled with creatures as far as the farthest eye could see. All at once the spotlights came up on the stage. A slick cobra, in a black-and-white tuxedo, slithered up to the mike. "Awwwww right!" he shouted. "Are your feet 'neath the seat? Is your face in the place? Have you got a smile as you dance down the aisle?"

The crowd stood and screamed, "Yeah, yeah!"

"Awwwwwww right! Here we go, Joe!"

The concert began. It was fantastic. The greatest bands in the land rocked and rolled until the ground shook with the beat. And finally it was time for the star that everyone had been waiting for.

"And now," cried the cobra, "introducing the superstar superband of all supertime —Funky Jan and the Animal Kingdom!" A gigantic cheer went up—they almost screamed the leaves off the trees as Jan and the band ran out. Jan waved happily to the crowd.

One after another she blasted out the songs that had made her a star. And finally she sang her new smash hit:

Can you help me find my song?
It used to be here,
Whispering right in my ear.

Can you help me find my . . .
Can you help me find my . . .
Can you help me find my song?

And the crowd went crazy. It was Jan's greatest triumph. She was at the top, just as B.L. had promised.

Suddenly, high above, a thick, dark shadow drifted across the moon—the shadow of a vulture. It flew toward the stage, casting its blackness wider and wider. The audience looked up and froze. The vulture swooped lower and lower, blotting out all the lights except one—the one that was shining on Jan. Then, with a rush of wings, it landed on the stage.

"Who are you? What do you want?" Jan cried.

"I want you. We have a bargain. I made you a star; now you belong to me."

Suddenly she recognized him. It was B.L.—the Devil himself. "You mean— No! I didn't mean that!"

The Devil smiled. "Too bad," he sneered. "Because I did."

"No!" shouted Jan. She threw the mike

at him and ran for her life. The crowd began screaming and fleeing in every direction. Jan leaped off the stage and raced through a field. In a ditch she saw an empty water pipe. In there, she thought. I can hide in there. He'll never see me in all the confusion. And she rushed inside.

But you can't fool B.L. Zebub that way. Oh, no. In a wink he had changed himself into a slinking polecat and slithered silently into the pipe after his prey.

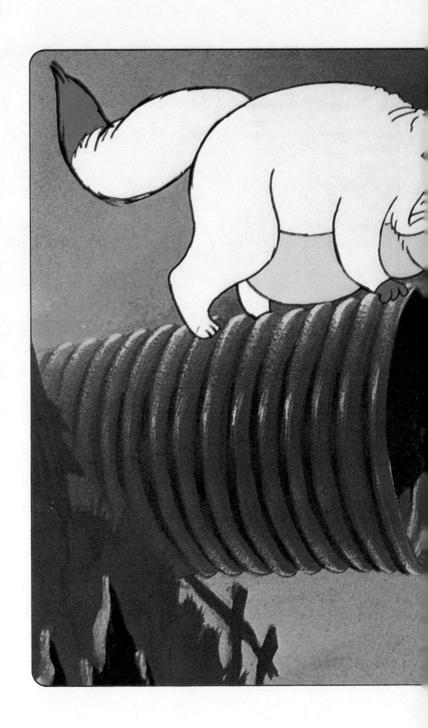

He came up closer and closer behind her. His paw reached out—but just in time Jan saw him. Out the other end she dashed. And then she was falling, falling, falling— right into a river. She swam underwater as far as she could. The Devil couldn't see her down here, she thought.

But of course he could—a sharp-toothed shark was gliding swiftly after her. Without a sound, it swam up behind her and opened its jaws.

Luckily, just then Jan managed to scramble out, and all the shark's jaws caught was a mouthful of water. Jan found herself at the edge of a thick wood. Trying not to make any noise, she plunged into the dark forest. Bushes scratched her. Vines pulled at her legs. She ran and ran until she could run no more. Finally she plopped down on a tree root and listened. There wasn't a sound. She was safe now.

Suddenly the root lifted! It wasn't a root! It was the Devil's foot! He had been waiting there for her all the time! With a flourish he reached into his pocket and pulled out the contract she had signed what seemed so long ago.

"According to our contract," the Devil read, "at midnight on the night of her greatest triumph, the party of the first part—that's you—agrees to surrender her soul, now and forevermore, to the party of the second part—that's me. Shall we go?"

"No!" said Jan, thinking desperately. "It's—it's—it's not midnight yet!"

"Pshaw. Technicalities. Oh, all right. You have until midnight. Then you're mine." B.L.'s sides shook with laughter. "All mine," he added. Then, in a puff of red smoke, he was gone.

My fans, Jan said to herself, they'll help me. They love me. They won't let Funky Jan be taken away by the Devil. She looked in the record stores, the concert halls, and the drive-ins. But it was no use. She was just plain old Jan now. No one recognized her anymore. And if they did, they didn't care what happened to her now. Even her old band had signed with someone new. She had no fans—and no friends.

After a while, she gave up. She sat down on an old stump, buried her face in her hands, and cried. What a dope she had been. She had been willing to give anything to be a star. Now she had nothing.

Then she heard a guitar playing. It sounded quite near. Maybe whoever it was would at least talk to her until it was time to go. She looked behind a nearby tree—and there, sitting up against the trunk, strumming a sad song, was Dan!

"Dan!" she exclaimed. "Oh, I'm so glad to see you!" She threw her arms around him.

"Jan?" asked Dan. He could hardly believe it was his old partner. Then he noticed her tear-streaked face. "Hey, what's happening? Something wrong?"

"Yes. I sold my soul to the Devil."

"No foolin'?"

"No. He's coming to get me at midnight."

"Wow. That's heavy."

Jan looked at her watch. It was just about time. "You'd better go," she said. "You don't want to be here when he comes. Good-bye, Dan."

Dan put down his guitar and leaped to his feet. He looked as if he had made a decision. "No!" he said. "He can't take you. I won't let him."

"It's too late," Jan replied.

And as if to prove her words, the earth began to tremble. A second later, B.L. and Weez appeared out of a puff of smoke.

"Ah, right on time. Ready, my little apple dumpling?" laughed B.L.

"Love it, B.L.!" exclaimed Weez. You're fantastic!"

"She's not going," Dan said.

"Heeeeeeey, she's got to. She signed a contract. It's all down in red and white."

"No! I challenge the contract! I demand a trial! This is a democratic forest!"

The Devil's face grew flaming red. His lizard eyes bulged. The buttons popped off his shirt. His ruffles wilted.

"Oh, oh. You shouldn't have said that," muttered Weez.

But all at once the Devil calmed down again. A sly smile crossed his face. "I like it! I like it!" he exclaimed. "Yes, you can have your trial—on three conditions. One: I pick the jury. Two: I pick the judge. And three: if you lose—I get both of you!"

"No!" cried Jan. "It's not fair!"

"Fair, schmair. It's your only chance. Take it or leave it."

"We'll take it," said Dan.

"Gooooood," laughed the Devil. He snapped his fingers. Out of the ground, one by one, came the jury. Dan's heart sank when he saw them: Richard Rat, who used to own a record company that cheated its singers; Les Leech, who used to be an agent who bled his singers dry; and Vicki Viper,

41

who used to be a big star until she lost her voice. She hated everybody—especially other singers. And the judge was none other than Weez Weezel.

"Court will come to order," Weez called. "The case of the Devil versus Daniel Mouse."

"Guilty!" yelled the jury. "They're guilty! Take them away!"

"Shhhhhh," whispered Weez. "Not yet." He held up the contract. "Did you sign this?" he asked Jan.

"Yes, but—"

"What's that? Speak up!"

"Yes, but—"

Weez turned to the jury. "Now," he instructed.

"Guilty! Guilty!" cried the jury.

Dan jumped to his feet. There was a huge lawbook on a stump in front of him.

"I object! We haven't had our turn," Dan said.

Weez looked at B.L.

"Oh, all right," said the Devil. "But hurry up."

Dan stretched himself up to his full

height. He wasn't going to give up without a good fight. "I say this contract is no good! Because—uh—because—uh—because she was too young!"

"She was old enough to sign," replied the Devil.

"Right!" cried the jury. "Guilty! Guilty!"

"Wait!" objected Dan. "I say this contract is no good because—uh—because—uh—because she was too small."

"She was big enough to sign," replied the Devil.

"You tell 'em, B.L.!" cheered Weez.

Dan tried once more. He hoped he could think of something good. "I say this contract is no good because—just a minute."

Dan and Jan leafed through the lawbook as fast as they could. "Here!" they cried all at once.

"That's it!" said Dan. "I say this whole trial is no good because the jury has only three members—and the rules say you're supposed to have twelve."

Behind him a cheer arose. While Dan had been talking, the creatures of the forest had been gathering to watch. They were all rooting for Dan and Jan. And they thought Dan might have the Devil this time.

"Pshaw," sneered the Devil. He snapped his fingers. Suddenly, before their very eyes, each member of the jury multiplied four times—and now there were twelve on the jury.

Jan's hopes disappeared. "It's no use," she murmured. "I'm so sorry, Dan."

"Anything more to say?" mocked Weez.

It looked like the end for Dan and Jan. There was nothing more they could do. Dan looked around desperately—and then spotted his guitar, leaning up against a tree.

"Yes!" he shouted. "I do have something—to sing!" He picked up the guitar and started to play.

Look where the music can take you
When you're getting low.
Look where the music can take you
If you let it go.

At first Dan sang alone. But then Jan picked up the beat and joined in. Then Boom Boom Beaver began beating his drums. Rabbit Delight and Pray Mantis grabbed their instruments. Bees began to buzz out the words. Spiders began to swing. Grasshoppers grooved. Butterflies boogied. Pretty soon the entire forest was singing and dancing, snapping their fingers, clapping their claws.

"Stop that!" demanded the Devil. But they paid no attention. The music got louder and louder. They danced and they sang. And then—believe it or not—the jury started dancing. They couldn't stop themselves. The music just carried them away. B.L. screamed at them, but the music was too loud and they kept right on. Behind the Devil's back, Weez jumped down from the judge's chair and boogied around the grass. Everyone was dancing. The trees swayed back and forth; the wind whistled the tune; even the moon and stars seemed to be bouncing to the beat.

Dan got up on a rock. "Your Honor!" he shouted. "I say that rock 'n' roll can save your soul, and a song from the heart beats the Devil every time!"

"One, two, three—and we agree!" sang out the jury.

"Cra—zee!" shouted Weez. "I declare you free! This trial's over, and so says me!"

A tremendous cheer came from the forest creatures. Dan and Jan hugged each other happily. They had done it! They were free!

Weez sneaked a quick look at B.L. "Oh, oh," he said. Steam was pouring out of the Devil's ears. His eyes were circles of fire. His fingers had grown claws. The grass was scorched under his feet. "Eeeeeeeeeeeeee," gulped Weez. "I think he's mad."

Then the Devil let out a ferocious roar. The jury shriveled up and disappeared. The ground opened up under Weez. "I'll deal with you later," said B.L.

"Oh, well," shrugged Weez as the ground closed over him.

B.L. turned to face Dan and Jan. "So I gave you a chance," he stormed. "And you beat the Devil. Well, I've learned my lesson. From now on, no more Mr. Nice Guy!" And

he vanished in a cloud of red smoke.

Dan and Jan walked slowly away. Jan had learned her lesson, too. From now on, she would appreciate what she had.

And here's something for you to remember if you ever happen to get in trouble with Mr. B.L. Zebub—a song from the heart beats the Devil every time.

SONGS

I've Got a Song

Music and lyrics by John Sebastian

I've got a song. It's my

time for sing — ing.

I've got a chance and that's

all I can ask.

E₇ groove

'Cause for to-day this is what I'm do- ing.

E₇ groove

My kind of thing is gon-na

E₇ groove

be built to last. _____

E₇ groove

I've got a love. He gives sup—

E₇ groove

— port and af- fec- tion.—

E₇ groove

His kind of love has got me

55

Fly- ing so fast. _____

The more I love, the more I

know a- bout him,

The more he loves me and that's

all I can ask. _____ Woh. ___

Can You Help Me Find My Song

Music and lyrics by John Sebastian

Can you

hear me—I'm the one that wanted most—

— to sing you songs. Now there's peo-ple

listen- ing,   but   some-thing's

mis- sing.   Can   you

see   me   though there's peo-ple all a - round—

—   I'm   so a - lone.   With-out   your

lov- in,   it all   means   noth-in'.

Can you   help me   find   my   song.—

Look Where the
Music Can Take You

Music and lyrics by John Sebastian

Look-in' for some-thing that there's

no set way to find. _____

You've got to list- en to your own —

— sec-ond mind. _____

You were a-fraid— you wouldn't be

strong en—ough a-lone._____

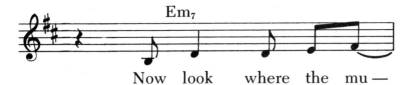

Now look where the mu —

— sic can take you,

If you let it go _____

Chorus

Look where the mu-sic can take you—

When you're get-tin' low _____

Look where the mu-sic can take you—

If you let it go. _____

You had a chance— to be a

star in your own dream. _____

Now you find that re- al- it- y is

bet-ter than   it seemed. _____

You   sold   your   soul—

_____   for   some   rock   and

roll. Now don't you see. _____

Noth-in' beats in- spir- a- tion, — and

in — spir-a — tion's free. _____